Amos
and the
Chameleon Caper

Gary Paulsen

Amos
and the
Chameleon Caper

CULPEPPER ADVENTURES

A YEARLING BOOK

Published by
Bantam Doubleday Dell Books for Young Readers
a division of
Bantam Doubleday Dell Publishing Group, Inc.
1540 Broadway
New York, New York 10036

ISBN: 0-440-41047-9

Printed in the United States of America

November 1996

10 9 8 7 6 5 4 3 2 1

OPM

Amos
and the
Chameleon Caper

Chapter · 1

Duncan—Dunc—Culpepper sat on the edge of one of the stiff, molded plastic seats at the bus station in Des Moines watching his best friend for life, Amos Binder, pace the floor in front of him.

"Cheer up, Amos. It can't be that bad."

"You haven't met her. My cousin Tiffany is a pain. She'll want us to have tea parties and play dolls with her. And another thing—she cries all the time. You never met a bigger sissy."

Dunc watched a bag lady poking through the trash can near the door of the bus depot. He pulled his suitcase a little

1

closer and turned to Amos. "It's been a few years since you've seen her. Maybe things have changed."

Amos put his hands in his pockets. "I doubt it. Tiffany's family is in the process of moving to Washington. They only invited us down here to hold her hand while they get everything settled. Boy, am I glad your parents said you could come with me. Imagine—spending the whole spring break taking care of Tiffany by myself."

"I don't understand. I thought you said Tiffany was the same age as us."

"She is, but wait till you see her. She can't even go to the bathroom without an escort."

"If you feel that way, why didn't you just tell your parents you didn't want to come?"

Amos sat down. "They didn't give me that option. My dad was still sore about the ice cream."

"Ice cream?" Dunc raised one eyebrow.

"Yeah. He'd been after me for a few months to rake the front lawn, so out

2

of the goodness of my heart—and also because he was withholding my allowance—I decided to rake the leaves last Saturday."

"What happened?"

"About noon, I heard Sergio's ice cream truck coming down the block. I'd been working steady for a good ten minutes, so I thought I'd buy me a triple decker and take a short break."

"Your dad was mad because you took a break?"

"No. He was mostly mad about the hole in Mrs. Johnson's windshield."

Dunc sighed and waited.

"I was all set to order—one scoop of pistachio nut, one of marshmallow fudge, and one scoop of my favorite, pizza swirl supreme. But when I got close, a telephone rang from somewhere inside the truck. I was pretty sure it was Melissa calling to ask my opinion about that deranged Australian dude we have to write about in English. What's his name?"

Dunc knew that Melissa Hansen was Amos's one and only true love. For years

Amos had tried everything he could think of to impress her. Nothing ever seemed to work out. Not even hiring a mariachi band and standing in front of her house waving a fluorescent HELLO MELISSA banner. If anything, she was less aware of him now than before. Dunc also knew that if Amos were the last human on earth, Melissa still wouldn't call him about an English assignment—especially in an ice cream truck.

Dunc sighed. "The paper was on Hitler, Amos, and he was Austrian, not Australian. And it wasn't an English assignment, it was for history class. Oh, and just in case you're thinking about doing it, it was due last Wednesday."

"That's the one. Anyway, I didn't want to bother Sergio, because he was busy waiting on some little kids. So I ran around and jumped in the passenger side to answer it for him. Melissa likes me to get it on that all-important first ring, you know."

Dunc nodded. He had given up trying to tell Amos that Melissa could care less

4

what ring he answered it on, since she never called him anyway. Amos could be stubborn about things like that.

"I had plenty of time and probably would have made it, but I forgot I still had the rake in my hand. When I reached inside I accidentally hit the brake release with the handle, and the truck started rolling down that little hill in front of our house and stopped in front of the Johnsons'."

"That doesn't sound so bad."

"The truck stopped when it rammed Mrs. Johnson's new car. And you know that fake ice cream cone Sergio used to have on the top of his truck?"

"Used to have?"

Amos nodded. "Last time I saw it, the top scoop was still sticking through Mrs. Johnson's windshield. My dad gave me a choice: Either get a night job or come to Des Moines and baby-sit."

"Did you ever answer the phone?"

"That's the worst part. It turns out it wasn't a phone after all. It was just a bell Sergio rings to attract customers."

"I think you made the right choice—about coming to Iowa, I mean." Dunc looked at his watch. "I wish they'd hurry up and get here. It's getting late."

"It may be a while. Tiffany's dad is some kind of big-shot politician. He said he'd come for us as soon as his last meeting let out."

A man in a badly stained suit who hadn't had a shave in days sat down beside Amos. "Hey, kid. Got a quarter? I need it to buy coffee."

Amos scooted to the other side of his chair and whispered to Dunc. "This guy smells, and I don't think he's ever seen coffee. Let's get out of here."

They picked up their bags and moved to the window at the front of the lobby.

Amos stared out at the metropolitan buildings. "I didn't realize Iowa had any big cities."

Dunc cleared his throat. "Des Moines is the largest city and also the capital of Iowa. Its population is approximately two hundred thousand. Chief exports are—"

"If I wanted a rundown on vital statistics, I would have—Dunc, look, that grandma is crossing the street in front of traffic."

A small, bent, elderly woman was attempting to fight her way between oncoming cars to cross the street.

They heard the squeal of brakes and saw the woman fall. Her cane flew into the air and landed near the bus depot.

The boys raced outside. A cabdriver was already helping the woman to her feet. Amos handed her the cane.

"Thank you, sonny." She tried to take a step and fell back against the driver. "Oh my. I can't seem to get my bearings. I must be a lot worse off than I thought."

The cabdriver pulled out his wallet. "Here, lady. Take this, it's all I have." He shoved a wad of money at her. "I can't be part of no lawsuit or I'll lose my job."

The woman looked at the money. "Don't worry about me. I'll use this money to go to the doctor and we'll pretend this little accident never happened."

"That's fine with me." The driver hurriedly stepped back into his cab and drove away.

Dunc picked up the woman's purse and brushed it off. "Can we help you get someplace, ma'am?"

"Goodness no. I'm on my way to see my doctor. His office is just up the street." The woman took her handbag and tottered down the sidewalk and out of sight.

Dunc rubbed his chin. "Hmmm."

Amos looked at him. "Now cut that out. Every time you make that stupid sound, it's a sure sign you're gonna get us into some kind of trouble."

"Amos?" Dunc led the way back to the curb. "Did you actually see the cab hit that woman?"

Amos shook his head. "No. I hate the sight of blood. I'm pretty sure I had my eyes closed."

"I don't think it hit her. I think that woman fell after the cab had already stopped."

"What makes you say that?"

"Lots of things. Her bright green eyes,

for one. It's hard to explain. It was like they were laughing at us. And another thing . . ." Dunc looked through the bus station window. "Amos, that man has our bags."

A thin man with tattoos covering both arms had their suitcases and was moving quickly to the back exit of the bus station. Dunc started running after him.

"Hiii-yaaa!"

A girl in a white karate *gi* raced past them. She gave the man a vicious kick in the middle of his back and a quick chop on the side of his neck. He dropped the bags and crawled out the door, groaning.

She turned to Dunc just as he got to her and stuck out her hand. "Hi. I'm Tiffany, Amos's cousin."

Chapter · 2

Tiffany led them to the entrance of an elegant apartment complex. The doorman held the glass door open. "Good afternoon, Ms. Tiffany. Anything I can do for you today?"

"Not today, Grimes, thank you."

Dunc elbowed Amos, whose mouth was still hanging open, and whispered, "I thought you said she was a sissy."

Tiffany pushed the button beside the elevator. "Dad's meeting went long, so he sent me to get you. Boy, am I glad you guys came. Things around here were getting a little boring. Do you play any sports?"

Dunc pounded Amos on the back. "Amos here is the checker king of our school."

The elevator doors opened. Tiffany held them while the boys stepped in. "No, I mean real sports. Are you on any teams?"

Dunc frowned. "Not unless you count the debate team. I'm the captain."

Tiffany looked disappointed. "How about martial arts? Judo? Kung fu? Karate?"

Dunc shook his head.

Amos finally found his voice. "Jim Gots Yu."

Dunc stared at him, but Amos ignored him and went on, "I'm really into it. It's one of those highly specialized forms."

The elevator stopped. Tiffany moved to a door with marble columns on either side and put her key card in the slot. "I don't think I've ever heard of that one. Is it new?"

She heard a yes and a no at the same

time. Dunc had said the yes. Amos glared at him. "It's one of those old Chinese ones. Very old. In fact, it's so old only a select few people in the world even know it still exists."

"Sounds neat. Maybe you could show me some moves later." Tiffany opened the door and scooped up a black-and-white cat. "Spats, you entertain these guys while I get changed." She pointed down the hall. "Your room is the third on the right. Make yourselves at home. I'll be right back."

Dunc waited until she was out of hearing range. "Jim Gots Yu?"

Amos shrugged and headed down the hall. "It was the best I could do on short notice. You don't want her to think we're a couple of wimps, do you?"

Dunc put his bag on one of the twin beds. "What are you going to do when she wants to see some of your moves?"

Amos stretched out on the other bed. "She'll probably forget all about it, and if she doesn't, I'll wing it. How hard can it be?"

"Look at this view," Dunc said as he pulled the curtains open. "There's a courtyard down there. The building is in the shape of a horseshoe."

Amos sat up. "Shut the curtains. People from the other side can probably see us."

"It's her!"

"Who?" Amos jumped off the bed and moved to the window. "A movie star? Don't tell me—Melissa is in Iowa."

"It's not her—it's *her*." Dunc was almost screaming. He pointed to the apartment directly across from theirs.

"I don't get it. It's only a gray-haired little woman."

Tiffany burst through the door. "Is everything okay? I thought I heard yelling."

Amos moved back to the bed and sat down. "To be fair, I really should explain something to you about my friend Dunc. He's crazy."

Dunc turned. "You don't understand. The woman in that apartment is the one who claimed she was hit by the cab."

Tiffany was confused. "Some woman was hit by a cab today?"

13

"That's just it," Dunc said. "She wasn't. She only pretended to be hit. She was dressed in rags as if she was real poor. The cabdriver gave her a whole lot of money so she wouldn't turn him in. But when I picked up her purse I noticed that it was made from alligator skin, which is really expensive. I think she's a con artist."

Chapter · 3

"Here's what we have so far." Dunc made a couple of notes in his pocket notebook. "An elderly woman pretending to be poor who lives in a classy building like this and carries an alligator purse . . ."

They had just sat down to lunch. Amos took the first bite of his sandwich. "She's probably visiting here, and her daughter from Cleveland gave her the purse."

Dunc ignored him. ". . . who only pretended to be hit, when in fact the cab never touched her."

Tiffany came back into the room. "I looked in the phone book. There are no doctor's offices anywhere near the bus station."

". . . and who lied about going to see her doctor," Dunc said smugly.

"Give the lady a break." Amos peeled a banana. "Maybe she's senile on top of everything else."

"Amos does have a point." Tiffany sat on the arm of the sofa. "How could you prove any of this?"

"Please don't ask him that." Amos moaned and closed his eyes.

Dunc looked at his notes. "First we need to find out her apartment number, and then we'll talk to Grimes, the doorman, and find out who she is. Then, if our suspicions are correct, we'll need to set up a surveillance network."

"A surveillance network?" Tiffany asked, scratching her head.

"I told you not to ask," Amos said. "He thinks he's some kind of detective. We really shouldn't encourage it."

Tiffany laughed. "Sounds like fun to me. How do we find out her apartment number?"

"That part's easy enough. Come on." Dunc led the way out the door.

"Wait." Amos grabbed an apple. "What about lunch?"

He was talking to air.

Chapter·4

"Which one is it?" Amos rounded the corner with Spats trailing behind him.

"I don't know." Dunc looked at the nameplates on the doors as they walked by. "It's gotta be one of these two. But from this side, I can't tell which. I guess we'll have to wait until someone comes out."

"I have a better idea." Tiffany picked up Spats. "The woman has already seen both of you. She might get suspicious if you hang around. Wait behind that plant over there."

Tiffany put Spats on the floor and let

him run off down the hall. Then she knocked on the first door.

A large man with bulging muscles, blond hair, and a thin mustache answered.

"Yeah."

"Excuse me, sir. I've lost my cat, and I was wondering if anyone in your apartment had seen him."

The man yelled over his shoulder. "Hey, Wanda. You seen a cat?"

A gorgeous redhead slithered up next to the man and shook her head. The man looked back at Tiffany. "Ain't seen no cats."

"Thanks any—"

The door slammed in her face.

Tiffany turned to the plant and shrugged. Dunc motioned for her to go to the next door. She moved to it and knocked. There was no answer.

The boys stepped out of their hiding place and helped Tiffany catch up with Spats.

"I don't get it," Dunc said. "I was so sure."

"Everybody makes mistakes." Amos took a bite of his apple. "I wouldn't let the fact that you tend to make them more often than anybody else—in the whole world—bother you."

Tiffany opened the door of her apartment and stopped. "You know, there could have been another person in that apartment."

Amos frowned. "I told you not to encourage him."

She went to the hall closet and searched through the shelves. "Here's what we need." She held up a pair of binoculars.

"Great." Amos plopped on the sofa. "My best friend and my cousin are turning into Peeping Toms."

"Come on, Amos." Dunc took the binoculars and headed for the bedroom. "This way we'll know for sure."

"You two should be ashamed of yourselves—spying on people like this." Amos followed them down the hall. "I mean, how would you like it if someone did it to you?" He sat on the bed beside Dunc, squinting out the window. "Do you see anything yet? Maybe we should take turns."

Dunc held up his hand. "Wait. There's the muscleman. Looks like he's leaving. Okay, now the redhead is going into another room. So far I don't see anyone else."

"Do you need me to watch for you now?" Amos moved closer.

"Bingo!" Dunc handed Tiffany the binoculars. "Take a look at that."

Amos jumped up. "What is it?"

Tiffany put the binoculars down. "I guess you were right. Now what?"

Amos grabbed the binoculars. "Now, we let *Amos* have a look." He focused on the window. It was the woman from the accident. She was patting her gray hair. Then she picked up her purse and went through the door, smiling.

Chapter · 5

Tiffany put the phone back on the receiver and sighed. "That was my mom. My dad and his secretary had to fly to Washington, and my mom is still meeting with her home care committee. She won't be back till late, as usual."

"Did she say we could order out for pizza?" Amos asked hopefully.

"Let's do that later. Right now, why don't you show me some holds?"

"Holds?"

Dunc looked up from writing in his notebook. "You know—*martial arts* holds."

"Oh, those kind of holds. Well, I would,

but shouldn't we take this opportunity to—to—"

Dunc stood up. "Why don't we use this time to go talk to Grimes?"

"That works for me." Amos headed for the door.

Tiffany shrugged. "That's funny. I didn't think Amos was even interested in the case."

"Don't let that empty look fool you," Dunc said as he and Tiffany hurried out to the hall. "Deep down Amos is really a detective at heart. He loves these things."

"What things?" Amos punched the elevator button.

"I was just telling Tiffany how much you love detective work."

"Yeah, it's right up there on my list with zits and liver."

When they stepped out of the elevator they nearly ran over Grimes. He was sweeping up a cigar ash from the marble floor.

He straightened and smiled. "Why, hello again. Is there something I can help you young people with?"

"As a matter of fact, there is," Tiffany answered. "My friends and I ran into a sweet little elderly lady from apartment thirty-five-B. We were thinking of taking her some cookies later, but you know how fussy my parents are about strangers. I was just wondering what you thought of her."

Grimes rubbed the back of his neck. "I think you're confused, Ms. Tiffany. The only elderly people in this building are Mr. and Mrs. Greenstein in twenty-four-A."

"Are you sure? Maybe she's visiting."

Grimes moved behind a counter and looked through his record book. He shook his head. "No visitors have been logged in for the DeFraud apartment."

"Is that the couple's name who lives there?"

"There's no couple. Ms. DeFraud is a single lady. She just rented the apartment last week. I don't know anything else about her except that she paid cash and asked not to be disturbed."

Dunc nudged Tiffany's shoulder. "It's probably our mistake. Come on, Tiffany, we really should get back to our bird-watching now."

"Right." Tiffany moved toward the elevator. "Well, thanks anyway, Mr. Grimes."

Amos followed. "We're going bird-watching?"

Dunc jerked him into the elevator and waited for the doors to close. "Of course not. You didn't want me to tell Grimes we were watching Ms. DeFraud's apartment, did you?"

"Are we still doing that?"

"Look, Amos, it's like this . . ."

"Something weird is going on in that apartment," Tiffany interrupted, "and we have to find out what it is."

Dunc looked at her appreciatively. "I like the way you think. It's rare to find someone who understands real detective work."

The elevator doors opened and Amos stared at Dunc and Tiffany as they walked down the hall comparing notes. "Scary is a better word for it," he muttered.

Dunc glanced back over his shoulder. "Did you say something, Amos?"

"Don't pay any attention to me. You two supersleuths go right ahead and work on your case. I've got some investigating of my own to do—in the kitchen."

Chapter · 6

Amos was dreaming.

A monster cab with hairy eyebrows and huge, pointed teeth was chasing him down the sidewalk, chewing up everything in its path. It was coming closer and closer, when suddenly Amos tripped over someone's grandmother. She stared at him with big, black binoculars, and when she had him in focus she started beating him with her walking stick.

"Amos, wake up." Dunc shook him again.

Amos grabbed his arm. "Save me, Dunc! She's killing me!"

"What are you talking about, Amos? Tiffany's been knocking on your door for the last ten minutes. She finally asked me to come in here and get you. Why didn't you answer her?"

Amos let go and looked around the room. "There was this grandma with binocular eyes who was . . ."

Dunc pulled the curtains open. "I warned you not to eat that whole gallon of ice cream on top of that footlong bologna and Swiss." He moved to the telescope Tiffany had set up the night before and scanned the windows of the apartment across the courtyard.

Amos rubbed his eyes and yawned. "Did you guys ever see anything last night?"

"Both women were in the apartment. So we know the older lady is definitely staying there. What we don't know is why they're trying to keep it a secret."

Amos leaned back. "So, what do you and my cousin have planned today—another fun-filled morning of invading other people's privacy?"

"No, that's why Tiffany was trying to wake you up. She has a surprise for you."

"Really?" Amos swung his legs over the side of the bed. "What is it?"

"I'm not sure you're gonna like it."

"Of course he is." Tiffany pushed the door open and stuck her head through. "But if you don't hurry, we're going to be late."

"For what?"

"I have karate class today, so I called and asked permission for you to come down and show us some moves. The instructor thought it was a great idea."

Amos lay back on the bed. "I don't think I feel so good." He looked to Dunc for help.

Dunc shrugged. "How hard can it be?"

"Try to hurry, Amos. The class will be waiting." Tiffany pulled the door shut.

"You were a big help." Amos scowled. "Now what am I going to do?"

Dunc focused the telescope. "The redhead is going out again. I wish you hadn't got us mixed up in this martial arts junk. Now we can't follow her."

"Would you quit worrying about other people? We have a problem here."

Dunc put the cap on the telescope. "I don't know what you're so worried about. You've seen hundreds of ninja movies. Just fake it and give them a good show. They won't know the difference."

"You think?"

Dunc nodded. "If you live through it, you'll have them in the palm of your hand."

Chapter · 7

"I think I've changed my mind."

Dunc peeked out through the dressing room door. "You can't change your mind, Amos. There are people out there waiting for you."

"Let them wait. I look like I'm wearing my dad's pajamas."

The instructor had loaned Amos his own extra *gi*—along with his black belt.

"What am I supposed to do with this?" Amos held up the cloth belt. "It must be six feet long."

"You wrap it around your waist and tie it off somehow."

Amos wrapped . . . and wrapped . . . and wrapped. "Now what?" He had a couple of feet left over.

"I don't know, but you better do something quick. The instructor is coming this way."

Amos stuffed the end of the belt down the back of his pants and headed out the door.

The instructor gave him a strange look. "Is there a problem?"

"Well, actually—" Amos started.

"No problem," Dunc interrupted. "Amos here just needed some time to meditate. It's the most important part of the program."

"Of course." The instructor led the way to the front of the hall.

When Amos stepped on the mat, the room exploded. Everyone jumped to their feet and bowed. Amos hesitated and then bowed back.

A smile crawled across his face. He stepped off the mat and everyone sat down. Quickly he jumped back on the mat. Everyone scrambled to their feet again and bowed.

He would have tried it a third time, but Dunc grabbed his arm and pulled him to the floor.

"Students, we are honored today by the presence of someone who has knowledge of the ancient art of . . ." The instructor looked at Amos.

"Jim Gots Yu."

"Yes, well, I'd like you to give him your full attention."

Amos jumped on the mat before Dunc could stop him. When the class was finished bowing, Amos bent from the waist and bowed back grandly with one hand in the air, then strode to the center of the mat.

The room was silent. Amos threw his shoulders back, hooked his thumbs in his belt and began, "My honorable teacher, the great . . . Meow Say Tongue, made me promise that I would never show these sacred moves to anyone except the truly dedicated." His eyes narrowed and he looked into each face around the room. "If there are those among you who are not true believers, I have no choice but to ask you to leave."

Dunc rolled his eyes.

No one left.

"Please watch carefully." Amos kicked forward with his right leg. Then he kicked backward. Then he jumped around in a circle. "All right, class. Now it's your turn."

Amos walked around, rubbing his hands together and watching. "Put your right foot in, put your right foot out, put your right foot in and shake it all about. . . ."

"Oh brother," Dunc muttered under his breath. "He's got them doing the Hokey Pokey."

Chapter · 8

Dunc was waiting outside the dressing room when Amos finally came through the door. "What took you so long?"

"Autographs. I could hardly get away, they're all so crazy about me."

Dunc shook his head. "You're amazing, Amos."

"I know. Sometimes I even amaze myself. Who would have thought that I had this incredible ability? I'm thinking of starting my own studio when we get home."

Dunc looked at him. "Amos, you made the whole thing up."

"What did he make up?" Tiffany walked up behind them.

Amos coughed. "It's not important. Do you want me to call a cab?"

Tiffany followed him out to the sidewalk. "It's a nice day. Why don't we walk?"

Dunc saw a powder-blue Cadillac whip into a parking spot up the street. His eyes widened. "Everybody act casual."

Amos looked around. "What's the matter?"

"It's them. The man and woman from apartment thirty-five-B."

They watched the redhead go into a department store with a sign above the door that said BERTINELLY'S FINE CLOTHES AND JEWELRY.

Amos made a face. "It's a free country, you know. Going shopping wasn't a crime last time I checked."

"Amos is right." Tiffany moved down the sidewalk. "It's a free country. Let's follow her and see what she's up to."

Amos groaned. "It isn't fair. One Sherlock Holmes is enough for anybody. Why do I have to get stuck with two of them?"

Dunc pulled him down the street. "Come on, Amos. We might be missing something."

"You're breaking my heart."

When they got to the door, Tiffany stopped. "We need a plan. I know—if anyone asks, we're looking for a gift for my mother's birthday."

Dunc and Amos nodded and followed her inside. The store obviously catered to the more affluent people in town. The floors were carpeted, and glass chandeliers hung from the ceiling.

A saleswoman met them just inside the door. "May I help you—children?" She put her nose in the air.

Amos spoke first. "We're buying a gift."

"Ahhh." The woman seemed bored.

"It's for our great-aunt Gertrude—rest her soul."

The woman looked at him. "You're buying a present for a dead person?"

"Have you got a problem with that?"

"Well, I . . . no, of course not."

"Good." Amos moved to the jewelry counter. "Because she likes diamonds—big diamonds."

The woman led Amos to a glass showcase. Tiffany and Dunc pretended to look at the cashmere sweaters a few feet away. The redhead wasn't anywhere in sight.

From the back dressing room an elderly woman with bright green eyes tottered by, carrying a large alligator bag.

They watched her go out the door, get into the blue cadillac, and drive off.

A frantic saleswoman ran up to the counter. "Call the police! Someone just stole several expensive outfits and a diamond necklace!"

The clerk behind the counter dialed the number. "Do you have a description of the thief?"

The saleswoman seemed confused. "A nice-looking woman with long red hair went in to try on some clothes. She was in there such a long time I went to check on her. But when I opened the door, she had completely disappeared."

Dunc grabbed Amos. "We better go now."

"But what about Great-aunt Gertrude?"

"Amos."

"I'm coming."

Chapter·9

"It has to be. How else could they have done it?" Dunc studied the window across the courtyard. "Don't you think it's strange that we never see the two women together?"

"I think you're out of your mind," Amos muttered. "We've been watching that window for days. If there was anything going on, we'd know it."

"I'm telling you, Amos. The older lady and the redhead are the same person. They have to be."

"I've got it." Tiffany burst in the door. "The librarian was very helpful. I only had to go back a few copies to one of last year's papers. Listen: 'Police have arrived at a dead end in their search for a cunning thief who is seemingly able to change identities at will. This ability has earned her the nickname Chameleon. She is wanted in five states for grand theft and fraud. This woman is a master of disguise and could even be your next-door neighbor. If you have any information as to her whereabouts, notify the authorities immediately.' "

"Well, I guess that takes care of that," Amos said. "If you think the redhead is the Chameleon, call the police and let them take care of it."

Dunc adjusted the telescope. "We're going to do that, Amos. Just as soon as we have some solid proof to give them." He looked at Tiffany. "Did you get it?"

She nodded. "It wasn't easy. Grimes hardly ever leaves the front area." She held up a key card.

"What are you two up to now?" Amos eyed them suspiciously.

"I asked Tiffany to sort of borrow

Grimes's passkey so we could get into thirty-five-B and take a look around."

"We can't break into that lady's apartment."

"Sure we can, Amos." Tiffany sat down beside him. "We've got it all worked out. I'll watch the front entrance. When I see her, I'll phone Dunc, who will be waiting in the fourth-floor lobby. Then he'll run down and knock on the apartment door three times as a warning."

"Hold it. If you're at the entrance and Dunc is by the lobby phone, who's going to search the apartment?"

They both looked at him.

Amos held up his hand. "No way. Forget it. Did you see the size of that blond guy? He could squash me with one hand. It's absolutely out of the question."

"We understand, Amos. Don't we, Tiffany?"

Tiffany nodded. "Perfectly. Of course, you might be giving up the chance of a lifetime."

"I know," Amos snorted. "The chance of

having my face flattened or swallowing all my teeth."

Tiffany went on, "I was just thinking about what a hero you'd be when you got home. You know, if you were responsible for the capture of one of the world's most elusive criminals. That girl Dunc told me about—Melissa—she'd probably go nuts. But I'll understand if you'd rather not."

Amos sat up. "I didn't say I wouldn't do it. I just said it would be rough."

Dunc winked at Tiffany. "Okay, here's the plan. . . ."

Chapter · 10

Dunc waved to Amos from the end of the hall. Amos took a deep breath, inserted the passkey, and opened the door. The apartment had about the same layout as Tiffany's, except there were no pictures or personal items anywhere. It almost looked as if no one lived there.

Amos crept past the kitchen and down the hall. The first bedroom door was open. A weight set stood in the corner, and a couple of suitcases were waiting by the door.

Amos made his way to the next bedroom. He opened the door and reached for the light switch. When he did, he touched a cold hand.

He tried to scream but it came out as a squeak. Then he noticed that the hand was attached to the arm of a mannequin. The room was full of them, all wearing different wigs and clothes. A large table stood in one corner with plastic faces, wig stands, and different kinds of makeup spread out across the top.

Amos was trying to decide what Dunc would want him to take for evidence when he spotted the alligator purse by the closet. He snapped it open. Inside was a sparkling diamond necklace.

He put the purse on his arm and started out of the room. Then he saw it—a nose with a wart on the end sitting on the makeup table.

Amos folded his arms and thought about it. "It would serve the two of them right if I slipped out of here and they wound up watching this room all night."

Using some gooey plastic glue, he pasted on the nose. In the top drawer of the makeup table he found eyebrows and lips. The bottom drawer had moles, ears, and scars. He pasted on fuzzy black eyebrows, fat red lips, and big floppy ears. When he was through with his face, he chose a short black wig. He barely had it in place when he heard the front door opening.

Someone walked down the hall and opened the bedroom door.

"Amos, are you in here?"

"Sure, Dunc. Right behind you."

Dunc turned. Amos was standing beside the mannequins holding the purse.

Dunc touched his face. "Amos, is that you?"

"How do you like the new look?" Amos grinned.

"You mean you've been in here playing all this time? I was getting worried that something had happened to you."

Amos tried to pull the nose off. It was stuck. "I wasn't playing. I was . . . experimenting."

Dunc looked around. "Look at all this stuff. It looks like the backstage of a theater."

Amos pulled at one of his oversized ears. "Can you give me a hand here, Dunc?"

Dunc opened the closet. It was full of expensive clothes, paintings, and jewelry. "You've done great work, Amos. There's enough stuff here to put the Chameleon away for life."

"Yeah, sure. Say, could you help me with these lips? I can't seem to get them—"

"Shhh!" Dunc held his finger up. "I hear something."

The front door of the apartment opened again, and they heard voices.

"It's them," Dunc whispered and scrambled inside the closet. "Hide!"

Amos moved behind the mannequins and froze.

The bedroom door opened. "I'll get it for you, Wanda." The big man with the mustache sauntered into the room and looked around. He scratched his head. "There it is." He moved to Amos and pulled the purse off his arm. The man frowned and gave him a closer look. "Boy, these disguises of yours are getting uglier and uglier."

"What's that, George?" The redhead stepped into the room.

"Nothing. I was just saying that maybe you need to lighten up on some of these getups. That one over there is the worst yet."

The woman looked at Amos. Her green eyes flashed. "You idiot. That's not a dummy."

Amos's feet started moving. He was running full blast toward the door. The problem was, he wasn't going anywhere.

The blond man held him in the air by the collar. "What you want me to do with him, Wanda?"

The woman rested her chin in her hand and studied Amos. "Don't I know you? Of course I do. You're one of the boys from the bus station." She half-smiled. "I never forget a face, you know. It's my job." She looked around the room. "Where's your friend, the polite, nosy one?"

The woman moved to the closet and threw open the doors. "Oh, now I'm disappointed. I thought surely you'd have more imagination than to hide in here."

Dunc shrugged. "You didn't give us much warning. If you want to go back out, I'd be happy to try again."

George pulled Dunc out by the front of his shirt and held the two boys dangling in the air. "You want I should toss them out the window, Wanda?"

"Now, George. Is that any way to treat someone as clever as these two?" Wanda tweaked Amos's pretend nose. "You boys really should be proud of yourselves. No one has ever gotten this close to catching me before. It's almost a shame you won't be getting any of the credit."

"If you really feel that way about it," Amos said, "you could—"

"Shut up." The big man shook him. "Let Wanda think or I'll stuff you down the garbage disposal—a piece at a time."

Amos winced. "That won't be necessary."

Wanda clapped her hands. "I've got the most delicious idea. Tie them up, George. We're packing."

"Where are we going?"

"We'll pull one last job in this town—maybe rob a bank or something—and arrange it so these two get blamed. While they're explaining, we'll have plenty of time to get away."

George stuck out his lip. "It'd be easier to toss them."

Wanda patted him on the arm. "I know. Maybe next time. For now, be a dear and put them in the other room. I've got to get ready."

George sighed. "You're the boss."

He carried them into the bedroom with the weight set and dropped them on the floor. Then he picked up two sets of heavy barbells and set one on Dunc's throat and the other on Amos's.

George pointed his finger at them. "No funny business. You stay put till Wanda says different." He pulled the door shut behind him.

"Can you move?" Dunc asked.

"I can hardly talk. How much do these things weigh, anyway?"

"I'd say about three hundred pounds apiece."

Amos shifted so that his Adam's apple didn't hit the barbell every time he spoke. "I don't suppose you have a backup plan?"

"I didn't exactly figure on this."

"Great. We'll be the youngest bank robbers in history. I wonder if Melissa will wait for me."

The door burst open and cameras started flashing.

"Dunc, are you all right?" Tiffany knelt down beside them. "When you didn't answer the phone, I got worried and called the police."

"What about me?" Amos squirmed underneath the barbell.

"Amos?" Tiffany pulled his wig off. "What are you doing in that disguise?"

"It's a long story. If it's not too much trouble, would you mind asking one of those police officers to get these things off us?"

A reporter took one end of the barbell that was on Amos, and a policewoman lifted the other. Then they did the same for Dunc. The two boys stood up.

Dunc rubbed his throat. "Thanks." He looked at Tiffany. "Did they get the crooks?" He ran to the hall and saw a policeman snap handcuffs on George and lead him down the hall. "Where's Wanda—the Chameleon?"

The policewoman shook her head. "Sorry, son, when we got here she was gone. Don't feel too bad, though. Thanks to you kids, we recovered several thousand dollars' worth of stolen goods."

Dunc scratched his head. "Gone? How's that possible? She was here the whole time. We never heard her leave."

"The only people here when we broke in were the big guy and you two boys—oh, and the cleaning lady. But she's gone now."

Dunc and Amos looked at each other. "The cleaning lady!"

Chapter · 11

"It's too bad you guys have to go home. I can't remember when I've had so much fun."

Dunc gave his suitcase to the man behind the ticket counter. "We had a great time too, Tiffany, but school starts Monday, so I guess we better get back."

"I don't care if I never go home." Amos slumped in his chair.

"What's wrong, Amos? Dunc and I gave you all the credit for finding the jewels and stuff. They even put your picture in the paper. You'll be a hero when you get home."

"Some hero. I saw that picture. I looked like Dopey from the Seven Dwarfs. Melissa won't even know it's me."

"That reminds me." Tiffany touched his face. "Does it still hurt where we had to use the kitchen knife to pry your nose off?"

"Only when someone touches it."

"Well, here's our bus." Dunc took the tickets out of his pocket and moved to the door. "Write and let us know how you like Washington."

"I'll do that. Maybe you guys can come up there and see me next year." Tiffany waved at them until they went through the door to where the bus was waiting.

Dunc stepped up into the bus and stopped so suddenly that Amos ran into him. "Hey, watch it," Amos said. "Don't forget that my face hurts."

Dunc stared at the bus driver. She had bright red hair and green eyes. She winked at him, pulled the door shut, and started the engine.

"Find a seat, boys—it's gonna be a long ride."

Be sure to join Dunc and Amos in these other Culpepper Adventures:

The Case of the Dirty Bird

When Dunc Culpepper and his best friend, Amos Binder, first see the parrot in a pet store, they're not impressed—it's smelly, scruffy, and missing half its feathers. They're only slightly impressed when they learn that the parrot speaks four languages, has outlived ten of its owners, and is probably 150 years old. But when the bird starts mouthing off about buried treasure, Dunc and Amos get pretty excited. Let the amateur sleuthing begin!

Dunc's Doll

Dunc and his accident-prone friend Amos are up to their old sleuthing habits once again. This time they're after a band of doll thieves! When a doll that once belonged to Charles

Dickens's daughter is stolen from an exhibition at the local mall, the two boys put on their detective gear and do some serious snooping. Will a vicious watchdog keep them from retrieving the valuable missing doll?

Culpepper's Cannon

Dunc and Amos are researching the Civil War cannon that stands in the town square when they find a note inside telling them about a time portal. Entering it through the dressing room of La Petite, a women's clothing store, the boys find themselves in downtown Chatham on March 8, 1862—the day before the historic clash between the *Monitor* and the *Merrimac*. But the Confederate soldiers they meet mistake them for Yankee spies. Will they make it back to the future in one piece?

Dunc Gets Tweaked

Dunc and Amos meet up with a new buddy named Lash when they enter the radical world of skateboard competition. When somebody "cops"—steals—Lash's prototype skateboard, the boys are determined to get it back. After all, Lash is about to shoot for a totally rad world's record! Along the way they learn a major lesson: *Never* kiss a monkey!

Dunc's Halloween

Dunc and Amos are planning the best route to get the most candy on Halloween. But their plans change when Amos is slightly bitten by a werewolf. He begins scratching himself and chasing UPS trucks—he's become a werepuppy!

Dunc Breaks the Record

Dunc and Amos have a small problem when they try hang gliding—they crash in the wilderness. Luckily, Amos has read a book about a boy who survived in the wilderness for fifty-four days. Too bad Amos doesn't have a hatchet. Things go from bad to worse when a wild man holds the boys captive. Can anything save them now?

Dunc and the Flaming Ghost

Dunc's not afraid of ghosts, although Amos is sure that the old Rambridge house is haunted by the ghost of Blackbeard the Pirate. Then the best friends meet Eddie, a meek man who claims to be impersonating Blackbeard's ghost so that he can live in the house in peace. But if that's true, why are flames shooting from his mouth?

Amos Gets Famous

Deciphering a code they find in a library book, Amos and Dunc stumble onto a burglary ring. The burglars' next target is the home of Melissa, the girl of Amos's dreams (who doesn't even know he's alive). Amos longs to be a hero to Melissa, so nothing will stop him from solving this case—not even a mind-boggling collision with a jock, a chimpanzee, and a toilet.

Dunc and Amos Hit the Big Top

To impress Melissa, Amos decides to perform on the trapeze at the visiting circus. Look out below! But before Dunc can talk him out of his plan, the two stumble across a mystery behind the scenes at the circus. Now Amos is in double trouble. What's really going on under the big top?

Dunc's Dump

Camouflaged as piles of rotting trash, Dunc and Amos are sneaking around the town dump. Dunc wants to find out who is polluting the garbage at the dump with hazardous and toxic waste. Amos just wants to impress Melissa. Can either of them succeed?

Dunc and the Scam Artists

Dunc and Amos are at it again. Some older residents of their town have been bilked by con artists, and the two boys want to look into these crimes. They meet elderly Betsy Dell, whose nasty nephew Frank gives the boys the creeps. Then they notice some soft dirt in Ms. Dell's shed, and a shovel. Does Frank have something horrible in store for Dunc and Amos?

Dunc and Amos and the Red Tattoos

Dunc and Amos head for camp and face two weeks of fresh air—along with regulations, demerits, KP, and inedible food. But where these two best friends go, trouble follows. They overhear a threat against the camp director and discover that camp funds have been stolen. Do these crimes have anything to do with the tattoo of the exotic red flower that some of the camp staff have on their arms?

Dunc's Undercover Christmas

It's Christmastime, and Dunc, Amos, and Amos's cousin T.J. hit the mall for some serious shopping. But when the seasonal magic is threatened by disappearing presents, and Santa Claus himself is a prime suspect, the boys put their celebration on hold and go undercover in perfect Christmas disguises! Can the sleuthing trio protect Santa's threatened reputation and catch the impostor before he strikes again?

The Wild Culpepper Cruise

When Amos wins a "Why I Love My Dog" contest, he and Dunc are off on the Caribbean cruise of their dreams! But there's something downright fishy about Amos's suitcase, and before they know it, the two best friends wind up with more high-seas adventure than they bargained for. Can Dunc and Amos figure out who's out to get them and salvage what's left of their vacation?

Dunc and the Haunted Castle

When Dunc and Amos are invited to spend a week in Scotland, Dunc can already hear the bagpipes a-blowin'. But when the boys spend their first night in an ancient castle, it isn't bagpipes they hear. It's moans! Dunc hears groaning coming from inside his bedroom walls. Amos notices that the eyes of a painting follow him across the room! Could the castle really be haunted? Local legend has it that the castle's former lord wanders the ramparts at night in search of his head! Team up with Dunc and Amos as they go ghostbusting in the Scottish Highlands!

Cowpokes and Desperadoes

Git along, little dogies! Dunc and Amos are bound for Uncle Woody Culpepper's Santa Fe cattle ranch for a week of fun. But when they overhear a couple of cowpokes plotting to do Uncle Woody in, the two sleuths are back on the trail of some serious action! Who's been making off with all the prize cattle? Can Dunc and Amos stop the rustlers in time to save the ranch?

Prince Amos

When their fifth-grade class spends a weekend interning at the state capitol, Dunc and Amos find themselves face-to-face with Amos's walking double—Prince Gustav, Crown Prince of Moldavia! His Royal Highness is desperate to uncover a traitor in his ranks. And when he asks Amos to switch places with him, Dunc holds his breath to see what will happen next. Can Amos pull off the impersonation of a lifetime?

Coach Amos

Amos and Dunc have their hands full when their school principal asks *them* to coach a local T-ball team. For one thing, nobody on the team even knows first base from left field, and the season opener is coming right up. And then there's that sinister-looking gangster driving by in his long black limo and making threats. Can Dunc and Amos fend off screaming tots, nervous mothers, and the mob, and be there when the ump yells "Play ball"?

Amos and the Alien

When Amos and his best friend, Dunc, have a close encounter with an extraterrestrial named Girrk, Dunc thinks they should report their findings to NASA. But Amos has other plans. He not only promises to help Girrk find a way back to his planet, he invites him to hide out under his bed! Then weird things start to happen—Scruff, the Binders' dog, can't move, Amos scores a game-winning *touchdown,* and Dunc knows Girrk is behind Amos's new powers. What's the mysterious alien really up to?

Dunc and Amos Meet the Slasher

Why is mild-mannered Amos dressed in leather, slicking back his hair, strutting around the cafeteria, and going by a phony name? Could it be because of that new kid, Slasher, who's promised to eat Amos for lunch? Or has Amos secretly gone undercover? Amos and his pal Dunc have some hot leads and are close to cracking a stolen stereo racket, but Dunc is worried Amos has taken things too far!

Dunc and the Greased Sticks of Doom

Five . . . four . . . three . . . two . . . Olympic superstar Francesco Bartoli is about to hurl himself down the face of a mountain in another attempt to clinch the world slalom speed record. Cheering fans and snapping cameras are everywhere. But someone is out to stop him, and Dunc thinks he knows who it is. Can Dunc get to the gate in time to save the day? Will Amos survive longer than fifteen minutes on the icy slopes? Join best friends Dunc Culpepper and Amos Binder as they take an action-packed winter ski vacation filled with fun, fame, and high-speed high jinks.

Amos's Killer Concert Caper

Amos is desperate. He's desperate for two tickets to the romantic event of his young life—the Road Kill concert! He'll do anything to get them because he heard from a friend of a friend of a friend of Melissa Hansen that she's way into Road Kill. But when he enlists the help of his best friend, Dunc, he winds up with more than he bargained for—backstage, with a mystery to solve. Somebody's trying to make Road Kill live up to its name. Can Dunc and Amos find out who and keep the music playing?

Amos Gets Married

Everybody knows Amos Binder is crazy in love with Melissa Hansen. Only Melissa hasn't given any indication that she even knows Amos exists as a life-form. That is, until now. Suddenly things with Melissa are different. A wave, a wink—an affectionate "snookems"? Can this really be Melissa . . .

and *Amos*? Dunc is determined to get to the bottom of it all, but who can blame Amos if his feet don't touch the ground?

Amos Goes Bananas

Amos has more than a monkey on his back. It's a gorilla. Her name is Louise—and she's in love with him. Dunc isn't much help. He's convinced Louise is the key to solving a really big-time case involving some assassins and a respected senator. Who will prevail? Dunc? The assassins? Or Louise?

Dunc and Amos Go to the Dogs

Anyone who knows Amos knows that in his case, dogs are definitely *not* man's best friends. Even his own dog, Scruff, growls and shows his teeth whenever Amos is around. Amos isn't exactly fond of Scruff either. But when Scruff gets mixed up in a dognapping scheme, Amos and Dunc have to spring him.

Amos and the Vampire

It's Halloween and Amos Binder's big sister, Amy, has a date with a real freak. She's always dating rejects, but this guy looks like he was rejected by the grave! He's got pale skin, dark hair, mesmerizing eyes, and an annoying tendency to disappear, and he wants to have the Binders over for a late-night Halloween snack. . . . Can Amos and Dunc stop the vampire before he starts to bite? Or will Amy and her man do a little necking she will never forget?

**Read the action-packed books in
Gary Paulsen's
WORLD OF ADVENTURE**

The Legend of Red Horse Cavern

Will Little Bear Tucker and his friend Sarah Thompson have heard the eerie Apache legend many times. Will's grandfather especially loves to tell them about Red Horse—an Indian brave who betrayed his people, was beheaded, and now haunts the Sacramento Mountain range, searching for his head. To Will and Sarah it's just a story—until they decide to explore a newfound mountain cave, a cave filled with dangerous treasures.

Rodomonte's Revenge

Friends Brett Wilder and Tom Houston are video game whizzes. So when a new virtual reality arcade called Rodomonte's Revenge opens near their home, they make sure they're its first customers. The game is awesome. But soon after they play the game, strange things start happening to Brett and Tom. Now everything that happens in the game is happening in real life. Brett and Tom have no choice but to play Rodomonte's Revenge again. This time they'll be playing for their lives.

Escape from Fire Mountain

". . . please, anybody . . . fire . . . need help."

That's the urgent cry thirteen-year-old Nikki Roberts hears over the CB radio the weekend she's left alone in her family's hunting lodge. The sender is trapped by a forest fire near a bend in the river. Nikki knows it's dangerous, but she has to try to help. When she reaches the bend, Nikki finds two small children covered with soot and huddled on a rock ledge.

Nikki struggles to get the children to safety. But she doesn't know that two poachers are also hot on her trail. They fear that she and the children have seen too much of their illegal operation—and they'll do anything to keep the kids from making it back to the lodge alive.

The Rock Jockeys

Devil's Wall.

Rick Williams and his friends J.D. and Spud—the Rock Jockeys—are attempting to become the first and youngest climbers to ascend the north face of their area's most treacherous mountain. They're also out to discover if a B-17 bomber rumored to have crashed into the mountain years ago is really there.

As the Rock Jockeys explore Devil's Wall, they stumble upon the plane's battered shell. Inside, they find items that seem to have belonged to the crew; including a diary written by the navigator. It reveals a gruesome secret that heightens the dangers the mountain might hold for the Rock Jockeys.

Hook 'Em, Snotty!

Bobbie Walker loves working on her grandfather's ranch. When Bobbie and her cousin

Alex head out to the flats to round up wild cattle, they run into the Bledsoe boys, two mischievous brothers who are usually up to no good. When the boys rustle the girls' cattle, Bobbie and Alex team up to teach the Bledsoes a lesson. But with the wild bull Diablo on the loose, the fun and games may soon turn deadly serious.

Danger on Midnight River

Daniel Martin doesn't want to go to Camp Eagle Nest. On the trip to camp, the campers' van crosses a wooden bridge, and the planks suddenly give way. The van plunges into the raging river below. Daniel struggles to shore, but the driver and the other boys are nowhere to be found. It's freezing, and night is setting in. Daniel faces a difficult decision. He could save himself . . . or risk everything to try to rescue the others too.

The Gorgon Slayer

Eleven-year-old Warren Trumbull has a strange job. He works for Prince Charming's Damsel in Distress Rescue Agency, saving people from hideous monsters, evil warlocks, and wicked witches. Then one day Warren gets the most dangerous assignment of all: He must exterminate a Gorgon.

The Gorgon howls as Warren enters the dark basement to do battle. Warren lowers his eyes, raises his sword and shield, and leaps into action. But will his plan work?

Captive

When masked gunmen storm into his classroom, Roman Sanchez and three other boys are taken hostage. They are hauled to a run-down mountain cabin, miles from anywhere. They are bound with rope and given no food. With each passing hour the kidnappers' deadly threats become even more real. Roman knows time is running out. Now he must somehow put his dad's death behind him so that he and the others can launch a last desperate fight for freedom.

Project: A Perfect World

When Jim Stanton's family moves to a small town in New Mexico, everyone but Jim is happy. There's something strange about the town. The people all dress and act alike. Everyone's *too* polite. And they're all eerily obedient to the bosses at Folsum Labs.

Though he has been warned not to leave town, Jim wanders into the nearby mountains. There he meets Maria, a mountain girl with a shocking secret that involves Folsum Laboratories, a dangerous mind control experiment, and—most frightening of all—Jim's family.

The Treasure of El Patrón

Tag Jones and his friend Cowboy spend their days diving in the azure water surrounding Bermuda. It's not just for fun—Tag knows that somewhere in the coral reef there's a sunken ship full of treasure. His father died in a diving accident looking for the ship, and Tag won't give up until he finds it. But when two tourists want Tag to retrieve some mysterious sunken parcels for them, Tag and Cowboy may be in dangerous water, way over their heads!

Skydive!

Thirteen-year-old Jesse Rodriguez can't wait to turn sixteen and finally be old enough to make his first skydive. But when Jesse and his friend Robin find themselves in the middle of a dangerous international situation, they may have to make their first jump a few years early!

The Seventh Crystal

Each day at exactly three P.M., Chris Masters faces two great challenges. First he races home, trying to avoid the school bullies who have made a career of beating him up. Then, once he's safely in his bedroom, he takes on another opponent—a computer game called The Seventh Crystal. Chris doesn't know who created the game, but he does know The Seventh Crystal is the most challenging computer game he has ever faced. Chris becomes obsessed with mastering the game. So obsessed that the game seems *real*—and then Chris has something much bigger than bullies to worry about.